Barrio TEACHER

Arcadia H. López

Arte Público Press
Houston
Texas
1992

This volume is made possible through a grant from the National Endowment for the Arts, a federal agency.

Arte Público Press
University of Houston
Houston, Texas 77204-2090

Cover design by Mark Piñón

Barrio Teacher / Arcadia H. López
   p.   cm.
Summary: Arcadia López describes her development from a childhood of poverty and immigration to the achievement of her goal of becoming a teacher in the barrio.
   ISBN 1-55885-051-1
1. López, Arcadia H., 1909– —Juvenile literature. 2. Teachers—Texas—Biography—Juvenile literature. 3. Education, Bilingual—Texas—Juvenile literature. [1. López, Arcadia H., 1909– 2. Teachers. 3. Mexican Americans—Biography.] I. Title. LA2317.L817A3 1992 371.1'0092–dc20
[B]   92–6876
                                                                          CIP
                                                                           AC

The paper used in this publication meets the requirements of the American National Standard for Permanence of Paper for Printed Library Materials Z39.48-1984. ∞

I dedicate this work to:

> my parents who gave me life and the values that make me who I am;

> my husband and the rest of my family who supported and encouraged my efforts;

> and my friends and mentors who kept the faith in me.

INTRODUCTION

As I write the Introduction to this beautiful autobiography of my dear friend, Dr. Arcadia López, barrio teacher, I am moved by a deep sense of respect and love.

I first met Arcadia about twenty-five years ago when we were both teaching first grade in the very first bilingual program implemented in the San Antonio Independent School District. We weathered hard times together during those early years as bilingual teachers. Native language curriculum was non-existent; we created our own. We had little research to guide us. But most difficult of all, many of our colleagues in the profession rejected us because of their lack of understanding regarding this innovation called *bilingual education*. We were able to endure those early years for one reason: our students were learning! Arcadia and I have never regretted our roles as "pioneers" in bilingual education.

During the summer of 1966, we were both awarded Fellowships to the University of Texas at Austin, and we shared a dormitory room for nine weeks. It was then that I came to understand and appreciate the qualities of this remarkable woman. We have shared a beautiful friendship ever since.

There are so many things about Arcadia that are special. She has never lost her love for teaching or her zest for life. She is as eager a learner today as she was in her youth. She cares deeply about the quality education of all children, but she is especially devoted to Mexican-American students. She has a keen mind and a loving heart. She bore no children of her own, but she has been a mother to the thousands of children who were fortunate enough to pass through her classroom. She is dedicated to her God and her faith.

Arcadia celebrated her 80th birthday recently. Her many friends gathered around her to celebrate her life. And well they should, for her life is one of courage and determination in the face of many hardships. This beautiful woman overcame a hearing impairment, poverty, and discrimination to become a dedicated barrio teacher of highest distinction. Her story will inspire everyone.

Gloria Zamora

Barrio Teacher

Prologue

How much I have lived, seen and felt! My eyes have focused on the beauty of this world. My ears have listened to its music, my heart to its poetry. My being has felt the grandeur of the human spirit, and it has sustained me in need. My hunger and thirst for knowledge and skills are an endless quest. The many changes I have seen, most for the better, a few hurting ones, have become a part of me. I refuse to dwell on the unpleasant, for I have resolved to make the most of the goodness that exists. These attitudes have been my recipe for survival.

Life has given my husband and me so much: health, education, friends, challenging and rewarding work, a comfortable home. I thank God for each day we are permitted to live in this beautiful world of ours. Life has not always been like this, as you will learn. But still we need to give back to life, to share the blessings with others. But wait, I am getting ahead of myself. Let us start at the beginning.

CHAPTER 1

Flight from Revolution

My first recollection goes back to early July, 1913. It is of my hanging on to my mother's skirts as she hurried to the town's prison. She was on her way to speak to the *comandante*, the commander, to beg for my father's release. Father had been talking against some of the revolutionaries and had been thrown into prison. Mother convinced the *comandante* to release him.

Once the ordeal was over, Father wanted to remain in Sabinas Hidalgo, but Mother knew better. She immediately asked him to get the cart and oxen ready. Into the cart she threw a few belongings and got me and my younger sister ready to travel, and off we fled, all four of us. That night we were on our way to a different life in the United States!

Mother was right! A few hours after we had left, there were loud knocks and shouts at the door of our *jacal*, the hut we shared with my aunt and uncle. Soldiers were trying to break in to take Father back to prison. My uncle and aunt assured them that we had left, and they were left in peace to write us about the narrow escape.

It took us eight days to get from Sabinas Hidalgo to Nuevo Laredo by oxcart! The northern part of Mexico is usually very dry, but during those July days, according to Mother, the rains had come down fast and furious, bringing about flash flooding. When we came to the Salado River, which is usually stone-dry, it was flooded with deep, rushing, murky waters. Father had to get down and guide the oxen to a section where the water was not over their heads. That was a frightening experience!

We finally arrived at the border and immigrated to the United States on July 10, 1913. In Laredo, Texas, my parents felt liberated, joyous and not entirely strangers. They had spent several months there on their honeymoon.

Father had no trouble finding work. The owners of cotton fields were waiting eagerly to find cotton pickers. Father was contracted to pick cotton near Dilley, Texas. His plan was to earn enough money to continue the trip to San Antonio, where he believed some relatives were living. Mother's relief at being in a country free from danger compensated for the hard work required of a housewife out in the cotton fields. She would get up at five in the morning, prepare breakfast, and, after doing the dishes, she would go with me and my baby sister out to the fields to help Father. Before the sun got too hot, she would walk back to the shack to prepare lunch. When lunch was ready, she would take it to Daddy. Then she returned to work indoors until the sun was friendlier. At that time we would go out again to help a little more.

Father has told me that I would try to help too. He would ask me why I wanted to help and my reply always was that I wanted a pink dress! Even as a three-year-old, I showed a preference for pink.

When Father had earned enough money, we continued on our way to San Antonio. We arrived in San Antonio on a terribly hot August day. Father carried my little sister, Mother walked beside him guiding me by the hand. We walked and walked, trying to find Father's relatives—in vain. My parents were at their wits' end, lost and exhausted. Then Doña María, a little old lady who made tortillas and sold them to make a living, spied them. She asked them what in the world they were doing out on such a terribly hot day with two young children. They explained. Doña María told them to forget it, to stop trying to find their relatives and to follow her to her house. She suggested we stay there until we found our relatives or found another place in which to live. God Bless that little old lady with the big heart! Doña María introduced us to the barrio, our new neighborhood. That was the beginning of life there for an immigrant family.

Daddy never found his relatives, who were actually living in Houston, but he found work as a barber. Much later he was able to open his own barber shop. Daddy rented an "apartment" when it became vacant across from Doña María in the same neighborhood. He considered himself so lucky that he invited his brother and sister in Mexico to come join us. They did, and we all lived together once again.

CHAPTER 2

Life in the Barrio

This place we called home was hardly livable, but we made do. It was a two-room structure in a horribly rundown condition in a row of similar dwellings. They were strung together to save space, so as to rent to more people. The *corral*, or complex, occupied about one third of a square block, fronting on the first block of San Luis Street and hugging South Laredo at one corner and South Concho at the other corner. It was shaped like a big capital *C* with a break in the middle to serve as a wide entrance, an entrance for the tenants who wanted to come in through the back. Each apartment had two steps at each front door. There was no sidewalk and of course, no grass. Toward the back of the *corral* there was a string of three smaller apartments and shacks which housed three flush toilets and two showers. Although Doña María's apartment and ours marked the entrance, ours was the only one that had a lean-to. This lean-to made our apartment unique. It became my sanctuary. I used to relax there on a wooden platform along one wall. When I started school, I used the opposite wall to write the words I was learning at school. My mother had allotted me that space to write on and no other. Sometimes I would invite neighborhood children in to play school. As the teacher, I would ask them to say the words I had on the wall.

We had a few pieces of furniture in that apartment. I remember a brass bed, a big wardrobe and a charcoal brazier for cooking in the middle of the kitchen floor. On a griddle over this brazier, Mother cooked the best sweet flour tortillas. Children in the neighborhood made sure to be around when the tortillas were ready. All of us really enjoyed them.

Mother kept the apartment as clean as possible, but there were a few things she could not control. The ceiling in the front room was made of canvas and had accumulated pounds of dust during the years. Finally one day, it collapsed on us and spilled dust all over. The kitchen floor had holes in it, and rats often ventured in to look for food, and once even bit my sister's toe. The roof leaked, and Mother would complain to the landlady who collected the rent. She told Mother that her house leaked, too, and when it rained at night, she slept under an umbrella.

I remember some of the other neighbors there. When Doña María moved out, the Portillo family moved in. There were four girls with whom we enjoyed playing. Next to this family lived a woman and her twelve-year-old son, Álvaro. He showed me how to fly a kite. I felt the thrill of seeing a kite high in the sky and the pull of the string on my hand.

At the corner of Laredo and San Luis lived Don Pedro, who ran a store. He and his wife had two grown-up daughters. The older one became my sponsor at religious confirmation. Her name was Elena. The younger one was Lupe, and she had the longest black hair. Lupe claimed that her hair was the result of using potato water as a rinse! Their father died from tetanus after having stepped on a splinter as he was tending to his horse in a stable. After his death, the rest of the family moved away, and we never heard from them again.

Doña Calixta lived next to them on Laredo Street. She had many children, but I remember only three of the girls: Paula, Maco and the one called "Canosa" (the gray-haired one). In the next two apartments lived Tacha, her husband, and daughter in one apartment and Tacha's mother, stepfather, sister and a nephew in the other. Tacha shared her fun activities with us. Her husband had one of the few cars in the neighborhood, and she would invite us to ride to the park and to the river for picnics. She was the one who had a nativity scene every Christmas. One Christmas, she moved it outdoors and one night even had the *pastores*, actors as shepherds, perform a miracle play. That night was a memorable, spectacular one, one that I will remember forever. The color of the players' costumes, the chants and rhythm contributed to the excitement. My young eyes drank it all!

In the smaller apartments in the back lived Mrs. Riojas and her only son. There was also a young woman living in one of those apartments who was expecting a baby and was making exquisitely beautiful baby clothes by hand. Many pregnant women in the barrio would start preparing clothes before the birth of their babies.

Next to us lived Eduarda and her common-law husband. She was childless and grew very fond of my sister, Isabel. Once in preparation for the month of May, she bought Isabel a white dress, a veil and wreath so that she could go offer flowers to the Virgin Mary. What she bought for my sister, Mother bought for me, too. Mother was a very fair person. After Eduarda moved away, Daddy's three other sisters and one brother moved to San Antonio. His brother and his family eventually moved to Houston.

One family in these apartments stands out in my mind: the Rivas family—Don Octaviano and Doña Reyes and their children Jacinto, Elías, Josué, Aída, Magnolia, Angélica and Margarita. Don Octaviano was a tailor by day and a music teacher by night. I used to visit when the music lessons were going on. I learned that music could be written by using notes. Margarita and I were in the same class in school and became lifetime friends.

In the end apartment facing Concho street lived a beautiful

intelligent family; several members worked for *La Prensa*, the Spanish language newspaper. Berta, the youngest daughter, was a blond girl who spent most of her time in a wheelchair. She had been striken probably by polio and attended school whenever she could. There were no special classes for the handicapped then. When Berta's family moved out, an Anglo single woman, who had a large goiter, moved in. She was the only Anglo who ever lived in our neighborhood. I do not think anyone knew her name or attempted to know it. But we remember her for her kindness. She introduced us to fruit salad and its goodness. Often she prepared a big bowl of fruit salad and gave it to Mother. One day she went to the hospital, and we never saw her again.

There was an elderly couple who lived in a small corner apartment. The wife used to work at the first Mexican restaurant in San Antonio. She would bring *tamales* home to sell to the neighbors. In my sleep-walking, I was always going to buy tamales from her. There is a saying in Spanish, *La que tiene hambre en tamales sueña* (She who is hungry dreams of tamales).

I am sure I am missing some of the *vecinos* (neighbors), but there were too many people moving in and out of our *vecindad* to remember them all and in the right time order. So many, many years have passed. It is difficult to know who came first and who came next and what characteristics they possessed which made us relate to them and remember them better than others. But, whoever lived there, lived in peace; there were no major incidents, no fights and no crimes.

Across the street, outside the *vecindad* proper, the Italians, who owned the whole block and the houses on it, were opulent in comparison to those in our complex. The Risicas, a mature couple and their grown-up sons—Bill, Sam, and Joe—and their married daughter, Rosa—married to Frank Gerioni—and Rosa's and Frank's children—Marie, Sam, Fannie and Tano—all lived in the big, white, two-story house at the corner of S.

Laredo and San Luis.

Because the Gerioni children's ages and ours matched rather well, we played together a lot. We developed two softball teams: the Johnson team—because they attended Johnson school—and the Navarro team—because we attended Navarro school. There were always enough children to have a good game. I was always the pitcher, but once I had to show the catcher how to catch and the batter struck me on the mouth with the bat. I shall never forget! I still have a lump on my lip and continue to have dental problems as a result of the accident. My mother just said, "Keep playing softball." No first aid! I was always competing with Sam Gerioni, running and jumping. And if there had been trees, we would have climbed them together.

Around the corner from the Risica-Gerioni place, on Laredo Street, there was an old adobe house where Don Jacobo, his wife and daughter lived. He sold medicinal herbs and *La Prensa* newspaper. Often my mother would send me to buy the newspaper from him. Don Jacobo knew we had come from Sabinas, so he would call me *la reina de Sabinas*, the Sabinas queen. What became of this family I do not know. Many families were displaced when urban renewal came in. That area is now the site of the downtown Holiday Inn in San Antonio.

Next to the Italians on San Luis Street was a four-room house. In it lived the Estradas—the widowed Mr. Estrada, his two teenagers, Fortino and Julia, and Virginia, my age, and Concha, Isabel's age. It was a treat to play with the girls in their home across the street. Their home was so much nicer than ours. They had good furniture. I remember once while playing there, I accidentally knocked down a beautiful hand-painted glass lamp with a beaded fringe around the shade. I was so afraid that we could not pay for the damage, but no one said a word.

Mr. Estrada was a good tailor and could provide for his family adequately, but he could not prevent the death of his two teenagers and the death of Concha, which followed several years later. We suspected tuberculosis. Tuberculosis was widespread. Whole families were wiped out. We literally saw neighbors cough themselves to death.

My maiden aunt was very attracted to Mr. Estrada. She would get all made up and go to visit him across the street. This was a reversal: the woman courting the man. I guess it was because his house offered more space for privacy than ours. Well, it was all in vain, he decided to marry a young girl.

Down the block on Laredo Street there was a bakery, a two-story building with an upstairs porch along its whole length, which served as a roof for the sidewalk below. The lower level contained the work space, ovens and the bakery. Upstairs lived the Sustaitas, a childless couple. They loved my sister, Isabel, and would take her riding in their car. We used to go to the bakery and buy *pan de dulce*, sweet bread. We, children, particularly liked the *marranitos*, gingerbread pigs.

Next to the bakery was the Elizondo grocery store and home. (At that time most store owners and their families lived in the back of or above their places of business.) Don Manuel and Doña Brigidita and their children—Matilde, José Luis, León, María, Josefa and Florencia—all helped run the store. We bought our groceries there. My sister and I went there for items forgotten when the grocery list was made and taken to the store. We looked forward to the *pilón*, usually a free piece of candy given to us when we bought something. We usually went for sewing thread #50, white or black. Mother made or mended all of our clothes and Father's towels for the barber shop.

Down by the bakery lived Doña Gumercinda, an elderly woman living alone. Supposedly, she had money hidden somewhere, money she did not want to spend. She also had lots of pigeons. Whenever someone was sick, Mother would send us to a buy a couple of pigeons from her, and the sick person would get my mother's pigeon soup. How times have changed! Now, we go to the supermarket to buy canned or boxed soup.

Next to Doña Gumercinda lived Genoveva, also an immigrant from Sabinas. She was a widow who had two sons and four daughters. My mother felt very close to Genoveva. She relied on her when she needed help. When Mother was ready to give birth to my brother, Santos, Isabel and I were sent to spend the day with Genoveva while the midwife did her work. This happened again five years later when my sister, Eloísa, was born.

Next to Genoveva lived two sisters who had classes for children in Spanish. We never attended, because we did not have the money to pay, and also because we felt we knew Spanish rather well and that what we needed to learn was English in a hurry to get acquainted with the outer world. And, of course, there was the public school two and a half blocks away, free!

What happened to Doña Gumercinda and the two ladies who taught classes in Spanish after the Catholic church collected enough money to start building a school on the land where they lived, I do not know. My family kept in touch with Genoveva until she died of tuberculosis. At one time her family and ours even shared a duplex.

To the north of our *vecindad*, we knew the Leungs, who had a grocery store at the corner of S. San Saba and Matamoros. The girls, Jenny and Lonnie, went to school with Isabel and me. Jenny moved back to China before the Communist Revolution. Nobody knows what happened to her. There were other Chinese families in the vicinity, enough to have a Chinese school on San Saba between Matamoros and Monterey Streets. The school was housed in a two-story building with four columns the length of two floors. The building had a beauty of its own. Perhaps it was because of its location among run-down living quarters and stores that its simple, clean lines stood out. This and the massive, palace-like structure where the landlady lived and which later became the Morales Funeral Home were notable sights in the barrio.

To the south, on Laredo Street, next to La Gloria, was "El Avispero," the wasp's nest, so called because many families lived there. Among them lived a woman known as *la güera*, the light-haired one, who made the most delicious enchiladas and sold them at a stand in front of the alley-like row of tiny shacks. None of this remains, perhaps for the better.

As I said before, we children got around the barrio and got to know it quite well. We never knew of any robberies or any kind of crime. We used to sleep outdoors during the summer and were not afraid.

There were several movie houses in the barrio. One was on Matamoros, and I remember during cold winter evenings Mother wrapped my baby sister, Eloísa, in a fake fur coat, and we all, except Daddy, walked to the movies for a night of fun. There was another movie house on Laredo Street near El Paso Street. We saw Rudolf Valentino in *Blood and Sand* there. Then there was the Guadalupe Theater on Guadalupe Street near Brazos Street. During the Depression we could go there for a penny. One by one these movie theaters were closed, probably because poor people could not support them.

CHAPTER 3

Childish and Adult Doings

Among the *chiquilladas*, childish doings, I played the role of demonstrator, the know-it-all. When some little girls complained to me that they could not swallow tablets or pills, I promptly ran into the house and got a bottle of laxative pills to show them how to do it. I swallowed pill after pill. Fortunately, I did not have any ill effects; at least, I do not remember any. Another time I got a piece of charcoal and showed them how to clean their teeth with it. After washing off the black stuff, our teeth appeared whiter. If the girls wanted to learn how to hit a ball, broad jump or crochet, I was willing to demonstrate, always the teacher!

Don't get me wrong, we children worked, too. Mother taught us how to wash dishes, clean house, iron, wash clothes, take care of the baby, sew and crochet. She taught us to share the chores. We took turns. When it was Isabel's turn to take care of the baby, she pinched her and claimed that the baby did not want her, so I got to spend more time with the baby. Isabel preferred to wash clothes and I preferred to iron, because I would always scratch my fingers on the wash board.

In the adult world in the barrio, there were other happenings which need mentioning. Whenever there was a death, *esquelas*, death notices in white envelopes bordered in black were sent. We, children, hated to see one for fear that a relative or dear friend had died. When neighbors had deaths of relatives, the women placed big lard cans over a wood fire outdoors to dye their clothing black. The wearing of black was an absolute requirement in observing mourning. The wake would take place in the home of the deceased, not at a funeral home. Many flowers bought at the market place were offered and the smell of the *azucenas*, tuberoses, was overpowering. The women did the crying indoors, and the men did the drinking outdoors.

There was a male individual who came to all the wakes in the barrio to get a chance at the bottle when it was passed around. One time he partook of the bottle too many times and got boisterously drunk. He resented being asked to leave, but under pressure, he felt he needed to say the last word. As he left he said, "Orgullosos porque tienen muerto," (You are uppity because you have a dead body).

There were two unforgettable periods of time which brought much happiness during those early years. One was of those moonlit, star-filled summer evenings when the neighborhood children got together to play games, sing and chase fireflies. Some games we played and enjoyed were Naranja Dulce, La Rueda de San Miguel, Los Colores, La Roña (tag), La Puerta Está Quebrada (London Bridge), Red Rover and Las Escondidas (hide and seek). The cool evenings, songs, games and rhythms gave me a feeling of happiness, a feeling of lightness, of being able to fly. There are no sweeter feelings than those happy moments of childhood. Poverty made no difference!

It took so little to keep us children happy. We were left free to entertain ourselves in our own creative ways. We had no radios, no television sets, no electronic games and no computers to keep us glued down. We had very few cars to take us places, and no loud music blaring away to distract us. We were active, very active. We were running, skipping, jumping, climbing, pulling, carrying and bending when we played our games. We were not lacking for exercise!

We ran when we played ball, and we ran when we played tag and hide and seek. We ran and ran. What exhilaration! No one told us we could get hurt, or perhaps we did not want to hear that.

We skipped for joy. We skipped and skipped. When the song said, "Brinca la tablita" (Jump the little board), we did. I still skip out in the back yard, where I hope no one sees me.

We climbed on everything we could except trees, because there were none to climb up on. It was fun! We pulled on a rope to see which team could pull the other across a line. Sometimes some of us fell, but we laughed about it.

We carried. We carried a playmate for some distance when two of us built a human chair with our arms. We enjoyed being carried more than being the carriers.

We bent when we played *La Campana* (the bell). We joined a companion, got back-to-back and locked arms. We took turns swinging back and forth in a bell-ringing movement.

We sang and swayed in our less strenuous games. Our ring games were melodious and very enjoyable. We sat down to play jacks with small stones and *La Gallina Papujada* (the puffed up hen) and other quiet games. We told stories, gave answers to riddles, chanted rhymes, played with dishes and dolls, and we made-believe a lot. We also collected soda bottle caps.

Our lives were peaceful. I don't remember ever having to hurry about anything. There was plenty of time to work, go to school and go to church.

Immaculate Heart of Mary Church and the Carmelite Orphanage and School were located nearby. They nourished our religious and social life. The Carmelites invited us to all their Christmas programs and often gave Mother fabrics which she made into school clothes. The sisters taught us catechism and prepared us for first communion. We attended all of the *jamaicas*, church bazaars, and when the priests built the school, they promoted plays which took place in the auditorium basement. There was a group of amateur players directed by Mr. Bernardo Fougá, who put on wonderful plays in Spanish. We never missed one. This was the beginning of my love for the theater. The theater was so important in our lives that I will mention it again and again.

Other happenings I remember are perhaps more important than our neighborhood events in the history of San Antonio. I remember when the Missouri, Kansas, Texas Railroad (MKT) came to San Antonio and built its station on S. Flores and Durango Streets. We, children, thought it was the most beautiful building. We saw it every time we went to deliver towels to Daddy, who had his barber shop across the street from the depot.

The building for freight covered from Durango to San Luis on S. Laredo Street. Many trucks came to the different sections of the building for pick-ups and deliveries. We could hear the iron curtains go up in the morning when it opened for business and down around 5:00 p.m. when the building closed. Today only a few tracks remain to remind us that the railroad business is not as lucrative as it used to be.

Before World War I, I remember watching the army trucks traveling south on Laredo Street. I was too young to know where they came from or where they were going. One day, one of the trucks crashed into the two-story building where the Italians had a store.

Another place I remember was the soap factory on S. Laredo. It manufactured the soap we called *jabón de automóvil*, trademarked Automobile. We would go there with Mother to redeem the coupons which came with the wrappers. This business is no longer there.

I remember the flood of 1921. We children were sleeping on the floor in the front room when we heard a woman's screams: "Wake up, wake up, there is a flood." We got up and Daddy ran out to find out what was happening. We were only about two blocks from the overflowing San Pedro Creek, nevertheless the flood waters did not reach us. In the morning we heard and read about the tremendous devastation. It was scary, but it led the city to build Olmos Dam.

• • •

Our barrio was isolated. The non-Mexicans who came in contact with us were few. The Italians across the street communicated with us in Spanish. So did the Anglo landlady, the Carmelite sisters and the Claretian priests. The only ones that did not communicate in Spanish were the teachers in the neighborhood school. We felt very comfortable speaking our language, except when we started our schooling with teachers who spoke only English. In spite of the poverty in the barrio, we were not unhappy until the Depression.

CHAPTER 4

Early Visits to Sabinas

The other periods of happiness in my life occurred when we went to visit our relatives in Sabinas during summers. It was the first time we went back to Mexico. Mother, my sister and my brother, who was the first-born in the United States, and I boarded a train and headed toward the border. The train engineers and the passengers were apprehensive because, across the river, there were still remnants of revolutionaries stopping and searching trains. We children were not too concerned about that. Riding in a train was a new experience, and we enjoyed it to the fullest. When the train reached Villa Aldama, my mother gave a sigh of relief that we had come that far without incident.

We hired a carriage to take us the rest of the way to Sabinas. The ride provided us with a beautiful scene. The hills we needed to cross to get to our destination were purple and beautiful towards the evening. Young eyes captured beauty so intensely!

In Sabinas we stayed with Mother's family, but we children visited Father's family daily, as they lived near an irrigation ditch which provided us with lots of fun. We would splash there to our hearts' content during those hot summer days. Another attraction there was a garden full of sweet smelling flowers. I shall never forget the fragrance of the jasmines and *reseda*, an Old World herb of the mustard family.

Neither can I forget my female cousins, who were much older than we were, and their preparations to go to the plaza. They sewed fabrics into beautiful dresses, and wore flowers in their hair and off they went to the plaza. To the tune of the music around the plaza went the girls in one direction and the boys in the opposite direction. This afforded them a good look at eligible partners. It was so romantic.

My maternal grandfather owned several fruit orchards. Every morning he would take us out to pick avocados, figs and pomegranates. We would come back laden with pounds and pounds of fruit. We would ripen the avocados which were not quite ready to eat by putting them into a barrel of husked corn. The figs we consumed readily, but the pomegranates gave us some trouble in cleaning them. I did not like them as much as the figs.

My grandfather's kitchen, separated from the main building, was always a source of delight. Hot corn tortillas cooked on a griddle on an elevated fireplace. We would spread *guacamole* (mashed avocado with spices) on the lightly toasted tortillas. How delicious they were. We would eat one after another!

Sometimes we would visit an avocado orchard along the irrigation ditch. We were amazed at the beauty of the avocado trees interlacing their branches with each other over the *acequia*. The avocados which fell from the trees were left on the ground or allowed to float in the water. Avocados were so cheap that the farmers were glad to get fifty cents for a hundred of them.

Before we left for home, Mother took us to the ranch which my grandfather owned near Vallecillos and where her brothers and sisters lived and worked. They had cows and goats. We learned to drink goat's milk and to ride in the oxcart. We ran and played a lot. I remember my male cousins liked to play *vaqueros* (cowboys), and I was always the calf. One day, one of them caught up with me and lassoed me and pulled tight. I can still feel the burning sensation of the rope around my neck.

We also watched our uncles burn the cacti enough to make it edible as fodder for the cattle. We also enjoyed watching our cousins take care of the goats. It was a carefree, delightful and glorious time for us.

CHAPTER 5

The Mexican Revolution

My parents left the Mexican Revolution behind and were glad to get rid of its reality. However, they continued to learn about it through the Spanish newspaper, *La Prensa*, and from refugees arriving in San Antonio from Mexico. My parents were really concerned about their relatives' lives and the devastation of the country.

The Revolution was truly scary. If it was anything as depicted in the movies, no wonder hundreds of people fled across the Rio Grande. I understand it was not as fierce as in the state of Chihuahua, but it was bad enough in the state of Nuevo León to force my parents to flee.

I remember my parents talking about a revolutionary hero who landed in San Antonio: Francisco Madero. He was destined to become president of Mexico. He stayed here for some time to plan ways to continue his opposition to dictator Porfirio Díaz's regime. Madero returned to Mexico, was arrested and killed.

Another person, Dr. Aureliano Urrutia, was a great surgeon who came to San Antonio and decided to stay to continue his practice here. Perhaps he had been in favor of Porfirio Díaz, a dictator in Mexico. Here he worked, acquired a rich and beautiful estate and settled down. I imagine there were other politicians planning strategies to stop the Revolution, but there were too many political parties vying to gain control. As one faction won, another faction brought it down. So it resulted in one president after another being murdered or deposed. I pieced all of this together from what I heard at home. I was really too young to comprehend all the implications.

From my father, I learned that José Vasconcelos belonged to the intelligentsia. My father thought that through Vasconcelos' writings, people would become aware of the danger of dictatorship and the futility of war, and perhaps find better ways of settling differences. Sometimes the pen is "mightier than the sword!"

Many men came to Father's barber shop for service and to talk about the Revolution. Their first questions were, "¿Cómo va la Revolución?" and "¿Qué dice *La Prensa*?" ("How is the Revolution going?" and "What does *La Prensa* say?"). The next question was, "¿A quién fusilaron ahora?" ("Who's been shot by the firing squad?") Many counter-revolutionaries and now refugees were shot to death.

I heard a lot about Pancho Villa, how he was trying to liberate the *campesinos* (farmers) and make their lives better. He was considered a sort of Robin Hood in Mexico. The U.S. government was trying to stop him from rampaging and pilfering the countryside. He operated mostly in the northern part of Mexico and on occasion went on raids across the border, in the area of El Paso, Texas. General John Pershing was sent to Mexico in vain to try to capture him.

I heard about the *soldaderas*, women who followed their fighting men to sustain them in their cause and personal needs. I have an idea that there were also some women involved in peace missions. I was told that there were even *niños soldados*, children that served as soldiers.

Some of my friends have told me stories about their families escaping the Revolution. Their stories were similar to mine. All these families suffered persecution at the hands of the rev-

CHAPTER 6

My Ancestors

Besides leaving the shooting part of the Revolution behind, I left my maternal grandparents, many uncles, aunts and cousins from both sides of my family. It was no wonder my mother needed to go back occasionally to visit her loved ones. She was affirming the family ties and exposing us to our cultural roots.

For us children it was the beginning of the mixture of two cultures: the culture of our ancestors and that of our new country. It was important to understand where we came from and what we were becoming. This cultural mix affected all we did, thought and perceived then and throughout our lives.

• • •

I hardly knew anything about my great grandparents, except that they all must have lived in the state of Nuevo León as pioneers some two hundred years ago. Both grandfathers were predominantly Indian and both grandmothers were predominantly Spanish. Both sets of grandparents each had fourteen children. Only six of my father's siblings survived to adulthood. My father was the youngest. Only eight of my mother's siblings survived to adulthood. My mother was the youngest of three girls.

My father's brothers and sisters varied in skin color, from very dark to blond. One brother, Uncle Jesús, looked like Santa

Claus; he had rosy cheeks, grayish blond hair and a round belly. My mother's brothers and sisters varied in skin color from dark to fair. Both my parents were *morenos*, brunettes. My father was darker than my mother. There was a great diversity among the two families.

I did not get to know my father's parents. My paternal grandfather, Santos Hernández, died when my father was a child. My paternal grandmother, Águeda Rubalcava Hernández, died when I was nine months old. She got to cuddle me, rock me in her arms and love me. My father was reared by his bachelor brother, Uncle Felipe, and a maiden sister, Aunt Isabel.

It is said that life for my paternal grandparents was hard and dangerous. When they had their first-born, a girl, they went to visit relatives living some distance away. On their way back they encountered a band of Indians. In their rush to get away from them, the baby fell from the oxcart. When the Indians disappeared, my grandparents went back to look for the baby and found her unhurt. The baby grew up, and I got to know her as Aunt Santos when she came to live in San Antonio.

I did get to know my mother's parents better. I remember my grandmother, Juanita Treviño Garza, as a woman with a round body and fair skin. She was gentle and sweet. She died in 1918. My grandfather, Don Inez Garza Chapa, was short, thin, wiry and dark. He owned a ranch near Vallecillos, where he raised goats and cows. He sent my mother to school in Villa del General Sauza, where she lived with an aunt while she studied. Grandfather left the ranch to be managed by his sons and their wives. My uncles tended the cattle and my aunts worked at home and grew small vegetable gardens in their unirrigated lands.

When grandfather moved to Sabinas, he built a home which consisted of two huge rooms and a detached *jacal* (hut) for a kitchen. The kitchen had a raised fireplace. First grandfather had a store, and then he began to make loans on mortgages. As

I said earlier, he owned some lots where he had avocado, fig and pomegranate trees. When he was a young man, he traveled to Texas to buy cotton. I believe he dealt in cotton futures. He also owned some mining stocks. He was quite a business man and a visionary! He foresaw that Sabinas would become a progressive town.

My grandfather lived to be ninety-eight years old. When he died in 1931, his eight sons and daughters met to learn about the will. My mother went from San Antonio. The will was worded in such a way that none of the inheritors got a whole property. It was one-eighth of the ranch, one-eighth of the house in Sabinas, one-eighth of the lots with the fruit trees and one-eighth of the stocks for each heir. It was a difficult situation. Mother's brothers and sisters started exchanging one-eighth of this for one-eighth of that. When my mother sold her eighths and took the U.S. exchange rate, she hardly had anything left.

Mexican families name their children after their close relatives or after Catholic saints. My mother was born on January 12, St. Arcadius' birthday. She was, therefore, named Arcadia and I was named after her. My sister was named after Aunt Isabel. My brother was named after grandfather Santos, Aunt Santos (Father's sister) and Uncle Santos (Mother's brother). There were too many Santos (Saints) in our family!

When the last child, Eloísa, was born, Mother put her foot down and said no more duplication. The tradition ended when my nieces and nephews gave their children new, Anglicized names.

CHAPTER 7

Mother

My mother, Arcadia Garza Hernández, was a remarkable woman. She had a strong sense of fairness and a stricter sense of morality. I knew she expected us to follow her example. She was firm but gentle. I don't remember her ever spanking us. She delegated that to Father. She always talked to us and explained things.

She quoted *dichos*, wise sayings, whenever appropriate. It was her way of teaching us. I still remember some of them and what they meant to me.

- *Dime con quién andas y te diré quien eres.* (Tell me with whom you go around and I'll tell you who you are). In other words, avoid bad company. A bad apple in a barrel spoils the rest.

- *Tanto va el cántaro al agua hasta que se quiebra.* (If you take a jug to water often enough, it will break.) Mother meant that, if you do something wrong, sooner or later you'll pay for it.

- *Del dicho al hecho hay mucho trecho.* (There's a lot of difference between saying and doing.) I understood Mother to say, actions speak louder than words.

- *No se puede tapar el sol con un dedo.* (You can't cover the sun with a finger.) I interpreted that to mean, you better not lie, because the truth will come out anyway.

- *Perro que ladra no muerde.* (Barking dogs don't bite.) That meant, don't talk too much about what you can do; let your actions speak for themselves.

- *Vale más sola que mal acompañada.* (It is better to be alone than in bad company.) That meant, either choose a good partner or go it alone.

- *Haz tu lucha y Dios te ayudará.* It meant, God will help you if you do your part.

These were only a few *dichos* that she used to repeat for our edification.

Mother was ahead of her time. She was the only one in the neighborhood who attended the Mother's Club at school, in spite of the fact that she did not speak English. Once she went to the school principal to complain about an unjust and cruel punishment he had given my brother. She could not tolerate that.

She was also the only one who dedicated time to read the daily newspaper and the weekly installments of *Romeo and Juliet* and other Shakespearean plays, *Chucho el roto* and other literature, all in Spanish. These booklets were sold house to house for about five or ten cents each.

She inherited her father's sense of business. She wanted to own property, but Father did not encourage it. She was so disappointed that, when lots were being sold in the Prospect Hill area, and she could not buy a single one. It wasn't until her children were working that she bought a house. What a pity! She could have been a sharp business woman. Isabel inherited her business sense.

CHAPTER 8

Father

My father, Francisco Rubalcava Hernández, was a barber. When we first came to San Antonio, he worked for the owner of a barber shop located on W. Commerce between Laredo and Santa Rosa Street, near the old Chapa Drug Store. As soon as he saved enough money, he started his own barber shop and rented a place for it across from the MKT depot on S. Fores Street. His work was the only means of providing for his family.

Father was quite different from Mother. He was not even tempered nor predictable. Occasionally, he did things in a grand style. Sometimes, he would forget to ask himself whether he could afford what he was doing or not.

One day he came home with a new phonograph and some recordings of operas. That was like having a new toy for him. He would buy us expensive shoes he could ill afford and sometimes he took us to places in a taxi. On one occasion when it had rained and rained hard, he sent me in a taxi to Our Lady of the Lake College, where I was taking some courses.

When I graduated from high school, he sacrificed to get me a beautiful white taffeta dress for the graduation exercises and a yellow georgette dress for the baccalaureate ceremonies. Father cared for us and loved us. Although he only demonstrated his love in spurts, we, children, always welcomed his generosity.

He was always talking about his school days in Sabinas. He

39

told us how the teachers taught by providing students with a list of questions and answers. The teachers asked the questions and the students answered them precisely as they were written, in a catechizing manner. Daddy was impressed with one question that had no pat answer. "How would you move the planet Earth?" Daddy said he was the only one who gave a plausible answer. "Have a strong and long enough lever and a place to anchor it to."

Father was always quoting some of the Mexican poets, such as Antonio Plaza and Amado Nervo. When I was at Sidney Lanier Junior School, he and I together read Juan Ramón Jiménez's *Platero y yo*. After that, it was a breeze to present an oral report to the class.

CHAPTER 9

School

I entered the neighborhood school at age seven, not knowing a word of English. The teacher did not know a word of Spanish. It was like being alone in the jungle, laughing for fear. I felt lost and scared and my parents could not help me. They did have faith in me, supported and encouraged me in my dream of becoming a teacher.

I remember well my first reader. The first page had a picture of a little boy and something written under it. It said, "This is Will. How do you do, Will?" I could understand that the writing was talking about the boy, but for the life of me I could not understand "How do you do?" as a greeting. The next page was just as bad, only the picture was changed to that of a girl named May. I don't remember how many times I failed the low first grade. An ear infection aggravated the situation. If I could not hear well, how could I discriminate English sounds?

Little by little I learned to make sense of the English language and made up for the time lost by going to summer school to catch up, even if I had to walk several miles to get to the school where summer classes were held. By the time I went to Sidney Lanier Junior School, I was pretty well caught up. Throughout my studies there, I was placed in the A sections, the fast moving classes. I was Club editor for *El Nopal*, the school's newspaper. I was selected for the Honor Roll. My classmates called me

Shakespeare and chose me as the girl with the most beautiful legs. What divergent characteristics! When I was ready to go to high school, the administration wanted me to remain at Lanier, which was also a high school. However, I realized I needed to have contacts with Anglo students; so I took my grade card and registered at Main Avenue High School.

What a shock and what frustration! To compete with native English-speakers was traumatic. I remember that in my freshman English class, I was assigned to write a theme on my most embarrassing moment. There were so many embarrassing moments, which one? How do you write a theme? I was so unhappy when I got my first grade of 70 in English, but, believe me, I learned to write well enough to get a 90 at the next grading period.

I had no difficulty with Spanish, history or math. My grades in Latin were excellent, varying from 97 to 99. There was a Latin Tournament every year in Austin, and I could not understand why I was never chosen to participate. I figured out later that I was too shy, not poised enough and did not have the proper clothing.

In Chemistry, I had a good partner, Ana, who was nimble with test tubes and burners. She loved manipulating tubes, measuring ingredients and performing the experiments. I hated anything that reminded me of cooking, so Ana proved to be the right half of the team. She did the experiments and I wrote them up.

My grades were excellent, and I was elected to the National Honor Society in my senior year. My parents were very proud. As I stated earlier, Daddy did not spare any expenses for my dresses for baccalaureate and graduation. My baccalaureate dress was a pastel yellow georgette dress and the one for graduation was white taffeta. Both were short; there were no caps and gowns then. This was the era of the flapper and the Charleston.

CHAPTER 10

Feelings as a Teenager

The teenage years were hurtful ones filled with introversion. Although I enjoyed studying and did well in my classes, I remained shy and uncommunicative. During the summers, I wanted to read and read and read. I read all of Jane Austen's novels, *The Count of Monte Cristo*, *Les Miserables* and everything I could get my hands on.

Poor mother! She had a hard time getting me to do chores. Worse, she was worried about my intense preoccupation with death. I used to feel my pulse to see if I were alive. My feelings were touchy, very sensitive, easily hurt. My youngest sister used to carry messages for me, because I was too shy to deliver them myself.

This period of growing into adulthood was extremely difficult, one filled with turmoil, confusion and deep emotions, of sleep filled with nightmares and days full of dreams. It was a time of sorting out ideas and behavior, right from wrong, truth from half-truth, practice from theory, reality from fantasy. I needed to get my feet firm on the ground, to tackle my deficiencies, my shyness, if I wanted to get ahead. I made up my mind to survive.

Poverty and my upbringing had much to do with my shyness. Going cold and hungry was no way to sparkle. Although both my parents were good communicators, excellent narrators of stories, they valued silence in children and believed silence was golden. In commenting about me they would say, "She is a lovely, quiet girl, so noble." *Noble* in the sense of being well-behaved. I realized I had to get out of my shell and become more assertive, but this took a long time to accomplish.

CHAPTER 11

Cultural Values

The culture that my parents brought with them and instilled in us was a source of reassuring vitality. It gave us a comfortable feeling, a feeling of safety, security, permanency. Its strength sustained us.

My parents kept in touch with relatives who were still in Sabinas and with residents here who were originally from Sabinas. Most of my father's relatives, group by group, finally made their way to San Antonio. Other people who came to San Antonio from Sabinas were the Rodriguezes and the Garzas, the soda water people. Once on their return visit from Sabinas, the Rodriguezes brought us some clay toy dishes that Isabel and I treasured very much. That was the way to keep close ties. Knowing and communicating with people from the same town gave us the feeling of belonging.

Oh, the stories mother told us about the persons and events in Sabinas and the ranch near Vallecillos! She told us of her early life, how from the ranch she was sent away to school to Villa del General Zauza where she stayed with an aunt. She related how her parents finally moved to Sabinas, built the house on Calle Juárez, used one huge room for a store, and how her brothers remained on the ranch to take care of the cattle. My grandfather was essentially a business man; he lent money backed by mortgages on land and houses.

Mother told of the people living in Sabinas—the De los Santoses, the Larraldes, the Montemayores—and their lives. She related how several persons reported seeing a fire, a glow seemingly coming from the ground, and how one man who was riding his horse one night saw the glow, dismounted and placed a stake where he had seen the fire. According to her story, the man went back in the morning and started digging where he had marked the spot with the stake and found a treasure! We, children, were wide-eyed, caught in the magical spell of her story.

Another story mother used to tell was one which made us feel that God had ways to intervene in human affairs. This one happened at the ranch. During an extremely hot and dry summer, a ranch hand was bitten by a rabid dog and became rabid himself. Not having medical help available, the neighbors locked him in a hut where they kept garlands of garlic. The man, being in the condition that he was, began devouring the garlic. When after some time the man's rantings and thrashings were not heard, the neighbors thought he had died. When they finally investigated, what a shock they had! The man was still alive and sane.

Mother sang a song over and over. I can still remember part of it. It went, "Ven a mi pobre cabaña que suspira y te extraña. Ven, ven mi amor." (Come to my humble cabin which misses you. Come, come, my love.) I looked, but could never find the music and lyrics to my mother's song. The knowledge that people sang and loved us gave us a feeling of continuity.

• • •

Father told us of life out in the mines. I don't think that he actually worked in the mines. What he did was accompany his older brother and help prepare the food over an outdoor fire. He told of ghosts and buried treasure, and my uncle would add his bit to the stories, as well. I could picture them sitting around the open fire eating their corn bread from an iron pan and sharing their stories. When they saw a glow nearby, they investigated, but they did not find anything. So convinced was father that there was a treasure there, that after thirty years, he decided to return to find the place. He felt that he and Uncle had overlooked removing an obstruction on the side of a hill, something like a door, and that was the reason they had not been able to find the treasure. He went all the way back to Sabinas, but he could not even find the mining site, much less the treasure. What he got was a treasure of experience!

• • •

Once or twice we indulged ourselves by having a piñata, especially for Isabel's birthdays, which happened to fall in the summer, on July 3rd. We would get a clay jar and decorate it with bright-colored tissue paper. We would also decorate the stick to hit it with. The jar was filled with candy, and the blindfolded children took turns trying to hit the piñata hanging from a clothesline. It was very difficult to do that because some adult always managed to swing the piñata out of reach, up and down and back and forth. But when someone did hit and break it, what a scramble for the goodies and what fun!

The Christmas season was a time for rejoicing. We attended church for *Las Posadas*, the pageant dealing with the nine days before Christmas, which was the time when Mary and Joseph traveled to Bethlehem where Christ was born. Seeing the procession was a source of happiness.

We helped mother make tamales. One of us mixed and kneaded the corn dough to the right consistency; another one of us washed and softened the corn husks. Mother prepared the chopped pork meat with spices for the filling. All of us spread the dough on the husks, spooned the meat in, rolled the whole thing up like a jelly roll, and placed the tamales in a big can to steam. The rest was easy—waiting for them to be cooked and then eating them soon afterwards. We usually gave some to our friends and neighbors.

Mother taught us to share our gifts. If she had nothing else, she took a plate filled with cookies and candies and gave it to each of our neighbors.

One Christmas, I bought small pieces of oil cloth, different colors and I cut out geometric shapes and pasted them on a larger piece of oil cloth to make a design for a small wall-hanging. I gave it as a Christmas gift to a friend, Simonita. Then, I thought that perhaps it was an insignificant present and felt ashamed. But when I went to my friend's house, I saw it on the wall. That made me feel better and reinforced my belief that a gift with the love of the giver is not bare.

On New Year's Eve we helped mother make *buñuelos*, crispy thin, sweet dough deep-fried in oil. Mother mixed the flour dough, and then she put a white, clean napkin on her knee and spread the dough into a thin round tortilla. She then placed the tortilla into the hot oil to fry.

• • •

What was important in our lives was our family values, our togetherness, our love for each other, our respect for life and our ability to celebrate life in spite of poverty. When one of us got sick, we were all concerned. Whenever anyone of us had an accident, we all tried to make things easier. When anyone did something outstanding, we all reveled, gave praise and offered congratulations. It was a good, exhilarating feeling!

CHAPTER 12

The Depression

I graduated from high school in 1928, a year before the Stock Market crash. The crash foretold of hard times ahead.

Of course, we did not lose any money during the Depression, because we did not have any in the bank or elsewhere to lose. Unemployment became rampant, and the people who continued to work earned a pittance. There were soup lines and many businesses were forced to close. Some teachers were being let go and the rest were paid in script. Times were tough, tough.

Few men could afford to get haircuts at my father's barber shop. Before the Depression, they got shaves also; but now they had safety razors and no money, so many men shaved themselves. Father earned very little during this time. All he could give mother was twenty cents a day to feed the family, which had grown to four children. Mother would buy corn dough and frijoles, and we would have tortillas and beans every day. These were hard times, very hard times.

We had always helped Daddy to earn money, but now we had to work even harder. We earned money at home by doing the finishing work on children's dresses—hems and embroidery—and by shelling pecans. In the summer, we went to pick cotton. That helped to buy clothes and supplies for school.

I was ready to go to college, but there was no money to pay the tuition. There wasn't even enough to take the bus nor to eat at the school cafeteria. So I walked the several miles to school and packed my own brown-bag lunch. Having to walk several miles was not conducive to a happy attitude. When I forgot my lunch, I had to suffer with an empty, aching stomach through classes. Also, I couldn't afford clothes like the other students and I felt out-of-place and completely isolated. This all contributed to a life of misery during my college days.

To make some money, Isabel and I sold our life insurance policies for a few dollars. That and a loan from the Federated Women's Club saw me through the first year at Our Lady of the Lake. The following summer, all of us, including Daddy, had to suffer the work of picking cotton. That was a hot, back-breaking way to earn money.

During my sophomore year, I decided to try something else: working during week days and attending college on Saturdays. I got on the substitute teachers' list, but that did not work well, because I had to rely on a neighbor's telephone. The neighbor was Mr. Sustaita, the bakery owner, who lived a half-block away. I looked for work elsewhere. I was hired as an office worker and I saved my part of the money to get a telephone installed and to pay for my courses. I also gave English lessons to one of the priests across the street and to one of the neighbors. Then I had more calls to substitute teach in the public schools on the west side of town, and I did a three week stretch at the Catholic school across the street.

When I went to Our Lady of the Lake, I was so focused on earning my B.A. degree so that I could start working and help my family that I couldn't allow myself to enjoy to the utmost the courses I was taking. My life was one of studying and more studying.

I majored in Math because it requied fewer language skills than other subjects. I minored in Social Sciences. Of course, I took all the courses required to earn a teaching certificate.

For a major in Math, I had to solve an intricate problem all by myself. I really don't know how I did it. I guess my endurance and determination helped. My Math teacher was very brief in giving explanations. She would send us to the chalkboard, and, as we struggled, she would offer a clue. We worked at the problems by ourselves. To think of all the hard work I put in studying algebra, geometry, trigonometry, and I never had to actually use those courses in teaching the elementary grades. In first grade, I taught plain arithmetic! Well, as one of my friends said, "All those studies helped you become a well-organized person." So be it!

The course which gave me a lot of frustration was Physics. It was taught by an absent-minded nun. When she lectured, she questioned every statement she uttered. She would say, "Physics is the science of matter and energy and the interaction between the two. Let me see. Is that right? It may be that other subject areas enter into it. I'm not sure. Mathematics, yes." She gave no concrete examples, and neither did we do any experiments. Of course, at that time she had no inkling of the physics involved in atomic and nuclear energy.

During my last year in college I worked in the library and the end was finally in sight. After six years of studying, I graduated in August, 1934.

I had done really well, mostly A's and a few B's. What a relief! But I did not imagine, as yet, the battle I would have to fight to get a teaching position.

Working for my Bachelor of Arts degree provided me several resources. One resource was friends who shared hardships with me. Another was the motivation to continue studying. And not least of all, was the pride I developed for my college, Our Lady of the Lake College.

After graduation, I applied to the inner city school district. The person in charge told me my English was not good enough. I thought, "Your Spanish is nothing." It took a long time and many people to intervene on my behalf before I was assigned to

joy!

After his retirement from the Air Force, Johnny started to work for a company that sold and repaired business machines: typewriters, cash registers, calculators and adding machines. He learned the business and liked it so well that he went into business for himself. He decided that it was safer and more profitable to have his business at home. He made the garage into his shop, where he worked and stored machines and supplies. He specialized in refinishing antique cash registers to get them in working order and to look like new. It took a lot of time and patience to do this kind of work, but it paid very well. He sub-contracted most of the repairs of the other machines, and he made calls to make deliveries and to bring in more business.

Johnny was a homebody. After his work, he preferred to stay home to relax and watch television. Occasionally, he went to the meetings of the former San Antonio members of the 141st Infantry Division. However, he was always ready and willing to drive me to my meetings that met at night.

A friend says that he treated me like a doll. In a way, that was true. I did not have to worry about washing dishes, putting clothes in the washing machine, taking clothes to the cleaners and grocery shopping. He did it all. When I was working on my doctorate, he took me to Luby's for dinner almost every evening, and when we did not go out, he cooked the evening meal.

We went to St. Paul's Catholic Church for Mass every Sunday and holy days of obligation. Sometimes we went to St. Mary's Cathedral in Austin, and after Mass we would have lunch at one of the cafeterias there. It felt good to be together and worship together.

• • •

I have been fortunate to have traveled extensively. I have visited many countries, have observed many people, and have found that people everywhere have more similarities than differences. They have the same basic needs. They may express their needs differently, because of their unique cultures, but they remain essentially human beings, seeking fulfillment and a better life for themselves and their families. If you find friendly, caring people in your community, you will find friendly, caring people in other communities.

In my travels throughout Europe, I have admired the European landscape—tall mountains, beautiful valleys and rivers. I have been interested in its historic churches, palaces and museums. I have enjoyed its symphonic and operatic music.

In my travels to the Eastern world, I have been impressed with the countries' ancient civilizations, with the people's friendliness and their down-to-earth life styles. Their temples and shrines have fascinated me and the people's skills in arts, crafts and handiwork have amazed me.

I loved India for its uniqueness, but its poverty disturbed me. In Bombay, Delhi, Jaipur and Agra, I saw many beautiful buildings very different from others in other parts of the world. Some of the buildings were forts; others were temples and others were hotels. Along side these beautiful buildings were pieced-up shacks, deplorable living conditions and many women with starving children asking for food.

Of course, the most outstanding building in India was the Taj Mahal. The Taj Mahal was breathtaking. It is the most beautiful palace I have ever seen: white marble with delicate borders of tiny pieces of colored marble. The water "canals" and long walks bordered by gardens leading to the palace give it an ephemeral, dream-like feeling.

The islands I have visited in the Caribbean, the Atlantic, the Mediterranean and the Pacific have a natural beauty beyond description. There are so many trees, shrubs and other plants with flowers of all shapes, sizes and colors, in clusters and in singles, on climbers and on upright plants. The vegetation on the islands is fantastic, incredible!

One good thing about traveling is that when you come back home, you appreciate more what you have. Often after returning from a trip, I found myself thinking, "San Antonio is beautiful in miniature. Its river and River Walk, its parks, its missions and its cultural heritage make San Antonio compare favorably with some of the best cities in the world!"

CHAPTER 14

More Schooling

Once I started teaching, I decided to start working on my Master's degree. I enrolled at the University of Texas in Austin, and during three summers I finished the coursework required for a major in educational psychology and for a minor in social sciences. I wrote a thesis based on my experience as a second-grade teacher, using case studies of some of my students. In August 1938, I earned my Master's degree.

Thirty-eight years after I had started teaching, there was an opportunity to join a special doctoral program offered by Nova University. Classes were held in Austin, San Antonio and in Fort Lauderdale, Florida, during two summers. I completed my doctoral work in a little over two years. The doctoral work was the most challenging, rewarding and self-fulfilling experience. It coalesced my experiences as a teacher and supervisor/coordinator with the latest educational research. My knowledge and skills were expanded tremendously. It gave me a push to continue striving for better ways to help children develop to their fullest potential and to improve or enhance teachers' skills.

If it seems that my doctoral work was a breeze, it was not. The course work and writing three practica kept me working from 4 p.m. until midnight. My experience as supervisor/coordinator suggested several topics for research and helped me write proposals for them.

57

One practicum was a group effort. Four of us decided to work together. I helped organize the practicum, made many suggestions and did most of the proof-reading. The other three participants wrote their parts and contributed well to the total effort. That was quite a learning experience in work relationships.

Workshops, seminars, conferences offered me practical learning. It was like going to school. I have never attended these activities without gaining some knowledge or skill. They prepared me to implement workshops of my own, and nobody can tell me that doing this is not learning of the best kind. You learn to size up your workshop participants, to provide for their needs, to answer their questions, to consider their evaluations of the workshop with an open mind. All these activities are learning experiences par excellence!

CHAPTER 15

Elementary School Teacher

As I have mentioned before, we were in the depths of the Depression when I started teaching at Navarro Elementary. The school was crowded; there were two shifts. As a new teacher, I got the afternoon shift, 1:00 to 5:00 p.m. My class had forty-two second-grade students. It was difficult to give them individual attention and to keep up with their attendance.

Back then a teacher served as nurse, speech therapist, counselor, parent and janitor, since there was a shortage of all these personnel. Several tragic things happened during these times. Students died of tuberculosis or congenital heart disease; they had speech defects; they became pregnant, delinquent—all because of lack of appropriate attention and care. It was heartbreaking to see all the misery and not be able to help much.

Of course, I was glad to have been assigned to Navarro where I had attended school for my elementary education. I felt I knew the community well, since I had lived in it. I hoped to be able to cope with many of the problems the children had. How could they learn without proper food, clothing and medical attention? I tried very hard to alleviate the conditions. It was a challenging situation and my efforts were rewarded. It was a good feeling coming back to my beginnings.

In my many years of service, I got to teach grades 1-5, but most of the years I taught first, my favorite grade. I learned so much by trying to provide for the children's needs and from the children themselves.

• • •

My years as an elementary school teacher provided me with many, many learning experiences, experiences that were enriching, experiences that led to great professional and personal growth. To my first principal, Mr. A.W. Eddins, I owe my calm, my skills in planning and my ability to execute plans effectively.

Mr. Eddins made his rounds of the classrooms every day. He entered, walked around quietly and observed briefly and then moved away just as quietly to the next classroom. Once every semester, he came in with his little black book for a formal visit and observed a lesson. Then he would call me in for a conference. He'd point out the strong points and suggest ways of improving the weak ones. He was the one who was the most responsible for the educator I am today. He encouraged and supported me in many diverse, subtle ways. He trusted me completely.

To Miss Jacksey Miller I owe my ability to relate other activities to teaching and my desire to join other education-related organizations and to render my services to PTAs and other associations needing help. She herself belonged to twenty-seven organizations and attended most of their meetings and functions. She had a tremendous capacity for such activities. Some teachers thought of her as a social butterfly, but her joy of living and giving was remarkable, endless. With her, every day was Christmas at Navarro. She was exceedingly kind and generous.

To Mrs. Leah Wells Young, the next principal, I owe my ability to put on assembly programs in an almost professional manner. She insisted that every teacher put on an assembly program every semester. With the help of my students, we worked on props, decorated the stage, made costumes and put on shows on such topics as the farm, school, nursery rhymes—with the near perfection worthy of any elementary school audience. We sang, danced, read, recited and acted. The children learned much and enjoyed performing, and the teacher barely survived the hard work.

It was when Mrs. Young was principal that Dr. Thomas Horn and his staff from the University of Texas, Austin, came to Navarro with an experiment in bilingual education. Being aware of the difficulties in teaching Mexican American children in English, I embraced the program wholeheartedly.

Because there were no third-grade teachers willing to take children in bilingual education classes, Mrs. Young could not continue with bilingual education. For this reason, after thirty-three years at Navarro, I asked for a transfer and got it. I went to Barkley Elementary where Mrs. Anna Zimmerman was principal. I taught there for a semester and learned how to prepare beautiful bulletin boards both for my first-grade classroom and for the hallway. During this time I had many visitors who came to see how I taught the bilingual education curriculum. I also gave several demonstrations both at the school site and at other schools. All in all, my experiences at Barkley were rewarding and pleasant. The reason I left was that I was asked to serve as a supervisor in the bilingual program.

CHAPTER 16

My Students

I have had so many students—some with serious problems, some with great potential. I remember better those that caused me great concern.

I had a boy named Alfred. He was a blond, wiry boy in my second grade. He was rebellious, belligerent, inattentive, hyperactive. Nothing seemed to penetrate his mind. He seemed uncaring. He was the type of student who when he goes on to another grade, the teacher gives a sigh of relief. Many years later, I had his sister-in-law in a graduate program I was directing. She told me he was doing fine. I guess he grew out of it without my help.

Herminio, another second-grade student, was a mixture of loving ways and misbehavior. In spite of his disruptive behavior, you could not help liking him. I wonder what happened to him.

Joe was in my first grade class. I tried to get him involved in wholesome activities. One Saturday, I took him to Brackenridge Park with my little nephew. We went by bus, since at that time I had no car. We had a wonderful time in the park. When I got home my coin purse was missing!

Mr. Eddins always gave me the children who had problems, thinking that if any teacher could do something, I was the one. He sent me a boy, Jesús, perhaps fifteen years old, who had just come from Mexico. He was tall and looked like a full grown man. He felt uncomfortable with first grade children. I had to get him a large enough desk-chair to fit him. I knew that it was a matter of transferring the skills he had learned in Spanish to English. I tutored him before school, during recess, lunch time and after school. He made great progress and after a few months I promoted him to the fourth grade. By the end of the year, his fourth-grade teacher promoted him to Lanier, the junior high in the barrio. This improved Jesus' self-concept tremendously.

Mike was another lovable boy, but hc seemed incapable of learning. His family would move back and forth from and to the Navarro School area. He was promoted regularly, automatically, in the other schools; but when he came back, Miss Miller, then principal, put him back a grade. On one such occasion, he asked, "Am I an elevator, going up in the other school and coming down when I return here?" Not long ago, I met him. He had joined the Marine Corps and served during World War II. His English was fluent, impressive, and he was terribly world wise. He had married and he and his wife owned a furniture store.

Jesse was a tall, lanky, skinny boy, too tall for his seven years. His walk reminded me of a spider. He walked wide, and his arms went up and down. Because his ears were big and sticking out, the children called him *conejo*, rabbit. He had a congenital heart, a heart you could almost see outside his chest. I went to Miss Miller, the principal, to ask her to find out what the San Antonio Crippled Children Association could do for Jesse. She informed me that the Association had a waiting list that would require Jesse wait two years to be considered for help. I decided to ask my personal doctor to assist. Dr. Saúl Treviño had Jesse admitted into Santa Rosa Hospital. Jesse would run away from the hospital to go home, time and time again; his mother would return him to the hospital, time and time again. It became impossible to keep him in the hospital, to give him the medical attention he needed. Soon afterwards, Jesse died,

died without the sustained attention he required.

Human beings are sometimes powerless. I felt so frustrated, so incapacitated, so restrained and so useless, forgetting that some things are better left to the Creator.

Mary came to school bent with pain and touching her stomach. Her mother seemed uncaring and not very concerned about her daughter's health. I was concerned. I referred her, one more student, to Dr. Treviño. He told me it was a chronic condition of the appendix. He was not eager to help, because he felt Mary's mother was a person not worthy of receiving assistance. In anger, I told him I didn't care about her mother, I cared about Mary, who had the misfortune of having such a mother. I cared about her getting well, being free of pain, being able to learn. Reluctantly, he saw that she had surgery. Mary got well and she and her family moved to Eagle Pass, where I understand she did well.

Recently, Mary recognized me at a meeting we both attended. She was so happy to see me. She told me she had never forgotten what I had done for her. She told her children about me, and they could not believe what I did. Mary made my day!

Another lovable child was J.G. His family moved around looking for farm work. He was intelligent enough to learn, but he was not in my class long enough for me to find out what was bothering him. One day I saw him playing with a knife, and I said, "Let me have the knife. I'll keep it for you." He answered, "If you want one, I'll steal one for you, Mrs. López."

A first grader, somewhat retarded, David was unable to stay near other children. He hit them or disturbed them. After grinning and bearing it for a few days, I contrived a place where he could be by himself. I provided him with crayons and other safe supplies to keep him busy. I labeled his place, "David's Domain." One day, while I was with a reading group, I saw him crawl quietly out the door. My heartbeat went wild. I thought he might run into the street and get killed, but I ignored him. He crawled across the hall to another classroom and tried to get another boy to do the same. When the boy refused, he crawled back to his domain.

Adelita was another first grader who was terribly emotionally disturbed. She would throw herself on the floor and scream and scream. (Her mother was in an institution for the mentally ill.) I trained the children not to be afraid of her, and they were real good about it, saying she was sick. The principal tried to help Adelita by bringing her Christmas ribbons for her hair!

There were some students who brought much joy to me. Among them was Leandro, who spent his third-grade year in my classroom. His thinking was beyond that of his companions. In discussing Thanksgiving Day, the children would express thanks for their parents, food, clothing, and shelter, but not Leandro. He was thankful for hospitals, schools, highways and for liberty and freedom.

Another student who did well was Jimmy Vásquez, now superintendent of the Edgewood schools. I had him in the second grade. I remember an incident reported to me by the only male teacher, Dámaso Hernández, who was always in the yard during recess.

Dámaso was deeply concerned about the future of our neighborhood students. He found ways to make children feel good about themselves, especially those who were having difficulty learning and staying in school, children at risk. He taught them about the Native Americans and their way of life, their culture. Students learned to use the bow and arrow, to dance Indian dances, to draw and paint pictures, to speak before an audience and to feel proud of themselves. All these activities they did to perfection. They performed in and out of school at different events and always got raving reports, standing ovations!

Well, to get back to Jimmy and Mr. Hernández. Mr. Hernández informed me that Jimmy, while at recess, came to him to report that a boy had spat in his face. Mr. Hernández asked Jimmy to remove the saliva from his face and Jimmy said he wanted to keep the evidence that what he said was true. Quite a lawyer, the youngest!

I still meet him quite often at meetings of an educational nature. He always greets me, "Maestra!" or "Profesora." He is quite the diplomat. He says how come he is getting older and I am getting younger. That is impossible, of course, but it makes me feel good, and I think that his managing the poorest school district in Texas brings him fame and stress. He has done so much to get equitable funds for poor districts!

CHAPTER 17

Bilingual Education

When Dr. Thomas Horn and his staff—Elizabeth Ott, Ann Stembler and Albar Peña—came to San Antonio looking for teachers to participate in an experiment, I was more than interested. The experiment called for ten teachers to teach English as a Second Language, ten teachers to teach in Spanish, ten teachers to teach traditionally the science materials adapted by the staff. All of us were to teach for forty minutes per day. I volunteered to do the Spanish. I was ready to try anything!

Previous to the bilingual education experiments, only about one third of my students performed well enough to merit promotion; another third was borderline and the other did not make it at all. So, I worked with the project wholeheartedly. I saw the change in the students immediately. They became more alert and they felt good about themselves. The first group of first graders demonstrated how well they did to the teachers in the project and to visitors who came to see what was to become bilingual education.

I was a bit disappointed when the staff came at the end of the first year to test for reading. All we had been doing was oral language development and some of that in Spanish. However, the experiment grant was continued and extended to the second grade, and my second group of first graders participated. When the project went to the third grade, no third-grade teacher wanted to take the project children, so the project had to be discontinued at Navarro. I asked for a transfer and got it.

I went to Barkley and taught a bilingual first grade class for one semester. At the end of the semester in 1967, I was asked to become a teacher specialist. My duties involved supervising teachers teaching bilingual education, supplying them with materials, doing workshops. It was something I enjoyed very much. Bilingual education was a turning point for me.

• • •

Recently I have been going through boxes of papers and have rediscovered the things I was involved in: the many classrooms I supervised, the many meetings I attended, the many visitors I took around to the different schools and the many progress reports I wrote. All were a record of my thirteen years in bilingual education with the San Antonio School District. All that, plus proposal and curriculum writing! I treasure the many friends I made and value my personal and professional growth.

When I retired from the San Antonio School District, I thought I would have a lot of time for volunteer work. No sooner had I been asked to join the Board of the Cerebral Palsy Association, when I was called to do some curriculum writing for the Intercultural Development Research Association (IDRA). Before I finished this contract, I was given another. Before I completed this second one with IDRA, I was called by Our Lady of the Lake University to direct a Title VII bilingual training program. Then I knew that I could never give up bilingual education, that bilingual education was and is a part of me.

When I was given the Trendsetter Award for Education by the San Antonio Area Association for Bilingual Education, I said, "In my 54 years as an educator, I've had many learning experiences in my effort to help children reach their fullest potential and to enhance or improve teachers' ways of teaching. I wish I had 54 more years to continue my endeavor." I meant every word of it. My commitment is steadfast, heartfelt and lifelong!

And I continue to attend all bilingual conferences, local, state and national. I also continue to serve on local committees, as judge in the San Antonio Area Association's Creative Writing contest and other cultural and art fairs at different school districts. The work seems endless, but it is satisfying.

CHAPTER 18

Retirement: The Last Hurrah?

In my thinking, I did not realize retirement would come so soon, after 46 years of service! It seemed like yesterday when I started teaching, but I did not resist leaving, as I knew there were other interesting things to do. So many memories! It was such a sad, sweet feeling!

The retirement celebrations given by my co-workers and friends kept things on a high note. Oh, the many parties, cards of congratulations, write-ups in the newspapers all were uplifting. My co-workers knew how to make me happy!

At the time of my retirement, I asked myself what it took to reach this point. The answer was a lot of living, all the involvement that influenced my becoming who I am. The joyous, rich, rewarding experiences which led me to feel I had the respect of my family, friends and peers. I hoped that these mutual relationships would expand from person to person, as in an endless chain. To know the meaning of our lives is to have reached the ultimate!

I remember retirement celebrations so well, because while the memories were still fresh in my mind, I compiled an album of mementos my friends had presented to me. The album cites dates, places and persons, and it also includes those items which can be placed in it. It provides me with warm fuzzy feelings whenever I look at it.

70

The celebrations began with a mini-conference for Area III of the San Antonio school district at Lanier High School on January 29, 1980. The "Bilingual Bunch" dedicated the conference to me and presented me with a corsage of small red roses. I was so thrilled I did not hear the applause or see the standing ovation I got, according to Mary Esther Bernal, my director.

But the biggest blast came as a complete surprise to me on Monday, May 5, 1980 at the San Francisco Steak House. Mary Esther Bernal asked me to go to a meeting with her. Yes, a meeting with over fifty friends who had gathered to honor me. Another corsage—yellow roses this time.

A mariachi group serenaded me and the celebrants. Rubén Sierra, a principal, wrote a poem dedicated to me. Someone else wrote a verse spelling my first name, with each letter complimenting me. The poem ended with, "ARCADIA, the teacher who means the world to us". The verse was put to music! Have you heard of so much to-do about a retirement? My friends are willing and capable of doing things in a grand way, and I loved and appreciated every minute of it.

On May 17, 1980, the San Antonio Area Association for Bilingual Education gave me a beautiful plaque in recognition of my dedication to Bilingual Education. I am very proud of it. There is no better feeling than knowing your peers value your efforts.

The next celebration was on May 22 when the J.T. Brackenridge faculty gave me a reception. The teachers bought a huge cake, and the teacher aides made one almost as big. They presented me with a gift—a necklace with an ivory pendant and ivory earrings to match. There was a huge sign across one entire library wall which said:

Felicitaciones en sus 46 años en la educación
Dr. Arcadia López, 1934–1980
Congratulations on a job well done!

The first and third lines mean almost the same. I felt so appreciated by my peers!

Then on Saturday, May 24, 1980, the Carvajal School teachers honored me at the home of one of the teachers. There was a buffet and lovely conversation. The two pots of African violets given to me and the party intoxicated me with such friendly feelings.

The next celebration took place on June 4, 1980, when the Title VII and ESAA Bilingual Advisory Committees honored a number of people, among them me as the only retiree. Again tribute was paid to me. This time the "Bilingual Bunch" presented me with a plaque which was inscribed with a poem I had written entitled "¡Hasta luego!" It reads as follows:

Se acerca la hora
de decir ¡Hasta luego!
y el tiempo de rendir cuentas
de lo mucho que ha pasado
y para saber qué ha quedado.
Me quedan muchos recuerdos
de niños adelantando
de colegas trabajando
de padres participando
de labores empezadas
cuidadosamente terminadas.
Recuerdos dulces que me darán aliento
por el cariño que he sentido
por el apoyo que he recibido
para seguir trabajando
siempre adelante y sin falta
con la cabeza bien alta
por lo que me he esforzado
por los niños.
¡Mi sueño realizado!

The hour has come
to say, Until later!
And the time to take account
Of so much that has happened
And to know what remains.
There remain many memories
of children going forward
of colleagues working
of parents participating
of works begun
carefully completed.
Sweet memories to encourage me
for the affection I have felt
for the support I have had
to continue working
always forward and without fault
with head held high
for all my efforts
for the good of children.
My dream come true!

What a beautiful feeling to think that my reflections on retirement were worthy of being inscribed on a plaque!

The last group celebration occurred on June 11, 1980 when the San Antonio Association of Supervisors and Administrators honored two retirees, one of them me. This group presented to me another plaque for distinguished services. I have had my share of honors!

A note from Dr. Felix Almaráz, Jr., became more important later than at the time I received it. It read:

Dear Doña Arcadia,
Best wishes to you upon entering
retirement—I know you will have
ample projects to attend—thus, you
are not retiring, but redirecting your
energies.

Saludos y recuerdos
Felix D. Almaraz Jr.

How true it turned out to be! He foresaw my continued
involvement in living fully. He was right!

CHAPTER 19

Some Honors

I have received several honors and have appreciated them very much for good reasons. I have felt surprised, humble, grateful and like crying. Recognizing the merits of a basically quiet person who talks about her accomplishments only when asked is extraordinary. The idea that some people are so perceptive and willing to recognize consistently good work gives me mixed feelings, such sweet sorrow. I feel so happy for the recognition that I can burst into tears, yet sad because others deserving of honors are not recognized. My sister tells me not to be concerned about that; people who work hard are appreciated and eventually recognized.

The honors that have become very meaningful to me seem to have come in groups: three in 1975, two in 1980, two in 1988, only one in 1987 and two more after that. The three in 1975 were celebrating the work I had done for the school district; the two in 1980 were in recognition of good work at retirement from the public school system; the two in 1988 were for lifetime commitment to bilingual education. The one in 1987 was for excellence in writing. The two, one in 1990 and one in 1991, celebrated my longevity.

The members of the Mexican-American Business and Professional Women's Club (MABPW) were the first to recognize my efforts by naming me Woman of the Year in 1975. It made me happy to know that the young members were aware of what an experienced teacher could contribute.

That same year another recognition was given me by the Women in Communications, Incorporated (WICI), for distinguished achievement. That honor was based mostly on my part in developing the Multimedia Learning System for Beginning Spanish-Speaking Children. This took place while I was working for the San Antonio Independent School District as curriculum specialist/supervisor in the bilingual education program. My part was mostly in preparing the teacher's manual. I especially appreciated this award, because the WICI membership was entirely non-Hispanic at that time, and it was unusual for it to recognize the efforts of a Mexican-American. I thank the MABPW for their enthusiastic efforts in breaking down barriers and submitting my resume for consideration.

The Golden Years Award in 1975 recognized my contributions to education. It was given me by Involved Mexican Americans for Gainful Endeavor (IMAGE). It was honoring several community people who were fifty years or older for their good work. This award was appreciated because the agency was not particularly involved in education.

In May, 1980, the San Antonio Area Association for Bilingual Education (SAAABE) gave me an award, recognizing my efforts and dedication to one reality: Bilingual Education. The inscription was written in Spanish. When I received it, Dr. Abelardo Villarreal was the president of SAAABE, and he had known my work since 1967 when we had worked together. I feel he had much to do with the award.

The next award came in November, 1980. It was awarded to me by the Ladies LULAC Council 282 for dedicated and unselfish contributions in the field of education. Here was another example of an agency not primarily involved in education recognizing the efforts of an educator. I feel a friend, a board member of the group, had much influence in selecting me for the award. She and I were members of MABPW.

Seven years passed without major awards. There were several certificates of appreciation for serving as a judge in school competitions and for serving on committees and holding office in different capacities. Then I wrote a piece on discrimination which I titled, "That Is Discrimination!" and submitted it to the Texas Association for Bilingual Education (TABE). The piece was selected as a winner with four other essays. I was given a framed certificate for excellence in writing. I appreciated this award because I had done much proposal and curriculum writing but not a creative piece. It made me feel fulfilled to know that an impartial committee thought my writing was good enough to be included in an anthology. The presentation took place during a dramatic ceremony called "Ever Vigil por Nuestros Niños," at which time the winners read their essays. There were speakers, a children's chorus and a mariachi group. The program ended with the lights out and lit candles held by everyone present while all sang "De Colores."

In May, 1988, SAAABE awarded me the Trendsetter Award in Education. It pleased me tremendously, and this time I became emotional. To think my co-workers really thought my efforts advocating bilingual education deserved recognition! Endurance, I have, and determination! I have exposed myself to a lot of learning experiences with the goal of helping students reach their fullest potential and to enhance or improve teachers' skills. But, I never thought I would be honored for that!

In October, 1988, the Texas Association for Bilingual Education (TABE) honored me for my lifetime commitment and contributions to bilingual education. Now this is a state organization recognizing me! The other honorees were Severo Gómez, Victor Cruz-Aedo, Elisa Gutierrez—the two were formerly with Texas Education Agency (TEA) and one still works there—Dr. Rodolfo Jacobson and Theodore Anderssen, who has written a number of books on bilingual education. I was among the truly great! These honorees were caring persons, persons who influenced others and who have made a difference.

At the ceremony, I wanted to make mention of my fifty-four-year quest for quality education for all students and teacher excellence. I wanted to state that I was accepting the award with humility for all the students and teachers who made it possible for me to receive it. But, the program for the luncheon did not allocate time for it. Just as well! After a sleepless night thinking about what I would say, I probably would have become nervous facing the hundreds of people at the luncheon.

There have been two other awards in 1989 and 1991. One was my induction into the San Antonio Women's Hall of Fame. That was in the education category. The other was my selection as the Woman of the Year by the *San Antonio Light* newspaper.

• • •

There have been many supporting actors in my life story. To begin with, there were my parents and my brother and two sisters, always encouraging. I never feared that the members of my family would desert me. I felt they stood solidly behind me. Of course, my husband always supported me in my work and in my studies. He made things easier for me to have time to do the things I needed to do. As to my extended family, it also gave me support, and there were many members of it. Both paternal and maternal grandparents had fourteen children each; so there were many aunts, uncles and cousins.

There is still a female cousin, on Father's side, Nieves Carrillo, who is a hundred years old or about to be. She is very alert and quite active. As a child I remember her when she was a young lady in Sabinas, making a dress and wearing it; I remember her placing flowers in her hair to go to the plaza, *a la serenata* (to the serenade). Her sewing skills became saleable when she and her family came to San Antonio in 1920. She worked in garment factories to support herself and several members of her family. She is now the sole survivor. She became so competent that soon she became a supervisor of the garment workers and later a designer. Every time she created a design, she earned a bonus. Her employer would not let her retire until the factory closed down, long after her retirement age. Financially she is in very good condition.

I must mention other supporting actors who helped me develop: my teachers, mentors, co-workers and friends. My fifth grade teacher, Eva Pirie, was outstanding. She was the kind of teacher whose ex-students come back to visit. Once when I was in high school, I went to visit her at Navarro School and she asked me about my classes. When I told her we were going to study one or two of Shakespeare's plays, she immediately offered me one of her volumes containing several Shakespearean plays and said it made no sense for me to buy the plays when she had the volume that had them.

One of my mentors was Mr. A.W. Eddins, my first principal, who put me on the way to becoming the teacher that I am. He took time to supervise me carefully, to write to me when I was in Austin getting my Master's Degree, and he allowed me to experience working with the P.T.A. He trusted me completely and gave me confidence. Another mentor was Dr. Josué González, the first bilingual education director under whom I worked. He guided me in the writing of proposals and in my projecting my knowledge and skills to others. Other mentors were Alberto Villarreal, who in his low-key manner, permitted me to come forward with my own ideas and approaches; Mary Esther Bernal, who recognized and respected my work; Dr. Gloria Zamora, who is always ready to suggest alternatives when I ask her help; Dr. Abelardo Villarreal, whose excellent Spanish influenced mine to become better and whose concepts on developing classroom materials are ahead of our times, materials which I hold as models; and Dr. Lucille Santos, who in her very competent manner, sees that I keep active and productive. And, of course, Dr. Blandina Cárdenas Ramírez belongs in this category. She suggested that I write this story and encouraged me to do so, saying it could become a social statement.

Among my supporting friends are Dr. Gloria Gámez-Solorio, who insisted that I continue to write this account, after she read the prologue and part of Chapter I and inspired me to go on; Frances Guzmán, who through her actions makes me think I am okay; Margarita Huantés, with whom I have had a lifetime of sharing mutual concerns and interests and of sustaining each other during difficult times; Hercilia Toscano, who has worked with me and has complemented my efforts; and Susie Greene, who was responsible for the typing of the first draft of this manuscript with her word processor; and Elsa M. Weiderhold, who typed additions and revisions, and gave the manuscript a professional look.

No woman is an island. There are so many other friends who lent their support and influence in some way or another that it would make too long a list to name them all, and perhaps there are some nameless benefactors. For all these supporters, thanks be to God!

EPILOGUE

I have done a heap of living! I have run a good race! I have tried to keep my outlook positive; my thoughts and feelings about people remain idealistic. I realize we all have our strengths and weaknesses, and only through strengthening our strengths and weakening our weaknesses can we hope for saneness, self-fulfillment and happiness.

In my struggle for self-fulfillment, prayer to the Supreme Being has helped. Prayer becomes more important as I grow older; increasingly, I need to express my praise and thanksgiving. I wake up praying, I go to bed praying, I pray at meals and I pray while driving. I am happiest when I attend Mass on Sundays and holy days, praying and singing praises. Prayer offers me the security I need to continue to live joyously.

My life has been touched by others; I hope I have touched others. What we have done for others is the ultimate test. If I have influenced a person or two to continue their struggle for self-fulfillment, if they can say truthfully, "I'm a better person because of her," then I will have lived a worthwhile life. ¡Hasta luego!